A  **ZIP IT!**

topps LEAGUE Story

· **BOOK THREE** ·

By **Kurtis Scaletta**

Illustrated by **Eric Wight**

Amulet Books
New York

For Byron,
who's been perfect so far
—K.S.

To Ethan and Abbie
—E.W.

PUBLISHER'S NOTE: This is a work of fiction. Names,
characters, places, and incidents are either the product
of the author's imagination or are used fictitiously, and any
resemblance to actual persons, living or dead, business
establishments, events, or locales is entirely coincidental.

Library of Congress Cataloging-in-Publication Data

Scaletta, Kurtis.
Zip it! / by Kurtis Scaletta ; illustrated by Eric Wight.
    p. cm. — (A Topps league story ; bk. 3)
    ISBN 978-1-4197-0436-9 (hardcover)
    ISBN 978-1-4197-0437-6 (pbk.)
    [1. Baseball—Fiction. 2. Superstition—Fiction.
3. Bat boys—Fiction. 4. Baseball cards—Fiction.]
    I. Wight, Eric, 1974– ill. II. Title.
PZ7.S27912Zi 2012
[Fic]—dc23
2012008406

Book design by Chad W. Beckerman

Published in 2012 by Amulet Books, an imprint of
ABRAMS. All rights reserved. No portion of this book may
be reproduced, stored in a retrieval system, or transmitted
in any form or by any means, mechanical, electronic,
photocopying, recording, or otherwise, without written
permission from the publisher. Amulet Books and Amulet
Paperbacks are registered trademarks of Harry N.
Abrams, Inc.

Printed and bound in U.S.A.
10 9 8 7 6 5 4 3 2 1

Amulet Books are available at special discounts when
purchased in quantity for premiums and promotions as
well as fundraising or educational use. Special editions
can also be created to specification. For details, contact
specialmarkets@abramsbooks.com or the address below.

ABRAMS
THE ART OF BOOKS SINCE 1949
115 West 18th Street
New York, NY 10011
www.abramsbooks.com

CHECKLIST

☐ **#1 JINXED!**

☐ **#2 STEAL THAT BASE!**

☐ **#3 ZIP IT!**

☐ **#4 THE 823RD HIT**

After the game I found a giraffe in my locker. I wasn't surprised. Yesterday there was a crocodile, and the day before that a monkey. All three animals were made out of balloons. The giraffe was the best one yet, with orange spots colored onto the yellow balloons with a felt-tip pen.

I was a batboy for the Pine City Porcupines. Balloon Day was coming up at Pine City Park, so Spike, the Pines' junior mascot, was learning how to make balloon animals. Not many people knew Spike's secret identity, but I did. I knew that Abby, a girl from my class, was inside the porcupine suit. Abby told me she wanted to be able to make any balloon animal a kid asked for, even if it was something crazy like a possum or an armadillo.

"What did you get?" I asked Dylan. He was the other batboy.

"I don't know." He opened his locker and pulled out a tangled knot of balloons. "What do you think this is?"

"A spider?" I took it from him and made it crawl up the locker. "I guess Spike remembers the time you saved that spider in the visitors' dugout."

"Spider? No way," said Teddy "the Bear" Larrabee, the first baseman. He took the crazy balloon thing from Dylan and said, "It's a . . . it looks like, maybe a . . ." He turned it this way and that, trying to think of something.

"A rabbit?" I suggested.

"Yeah, that's it—a rabbit. Spike knows you have a pet rabbit," Teddy said to Dylan.

"A mutant rabbit with about nine ears, maybe," said Wayne Zane, the catcher.

Teddy glared at him. "It's a rabbit with a bunch of carrots in his mouth."

"Just sayin'," said Wayne.

Someone tapped my shoulder. I turned around and saw our boss, Wally. He was the Pines' clubhouse manager. He tugged on his mustache. "Chad, I need to talk to you. It's important." He looked worried, and that made *me* worry.

Wally didn't have an office, but he had a desk in the corner of the equipment room. We went there now.

"What's that for?" Wally pointed at my balloon giraffe. I'd forgotten I was holding it.

"Nothing," I said. I set it down, and there was a *POP!* Wally practically jumped out of his chair.

"Gabbagah!" he shouted.

"Sorry," I said. I had set one of the giraffe's legs down on a thumbtack.

"It just startled me," said Wally, giving the giraffe the evil eye.

The rest of the giraffe was slowly deflating. I grabbed some tape from the desk and made a bandage.

"Here's the thing," said Wally. "I can't be here next Saturday. I need you to take on some extra duties. I picked you over Dylan because you know more about baseball."

"What do I have to do?"

"Lots of stuff. Get here early on Friday and I'll walk you through it."

"OK. Sure."

"One thing you'll have to do is make coffee," Wally said. "Lance Pantaño is the starting pitcher."

"Right." I knew that Lance drank several cups of coffee before every game, especially when he was pitching. I had never used the big metal coffeemaker in the locker room. It looked complicated. When coffee was brewing, the whole machine whistled and rattled like it might blow up. But I didn't want Wally to know I was scared. "I can do that," I said. "No problem."

• • •

"Did you ever figure out what that thing

is?" I asked Dylan, pointing at his balloon animal. We were crossing the parking lot after work. The Pines were headed out on the road, so we had to load up the bus after the game. It had been a long day.

"Maybe it's a mosquito," Dylan said. He made the balloon thing fly, then landed it on his arm and made slurping sounds. "Spike knows I'm going camping this week at Otter Lake."

"Sounds like fun."

Dylan liked animals. He probably loved camping out—all that nature.

"It's great during the day," he said. "I get to go hiking and swim in the lake. I just don't like it at night. It gets so dark."

"Don't you have a lantern?"

"They don't make a lantern big enough for how dark it gets," Dylan replied. "There might be bears out there." He shuddered.

We got to the end of the parking lot, where we usually split up and headed home.

"Guess I'll see you next week," Dylan said.

"Don't get eaten by a bear," I told him.

"Don't even joke about that!"

• • •

My giraffe was pretty much done for, even with my first aid. I kept it anyway, since it came from a friend. I set it next to the other balloon animals on my dresser. I didn't know why Abby kept giving me jungle animals, but they did look good together, even if the giraffe was the shortest one up there.

I thought about how Wally had reacted when the giraffe popped. He nearly jumped out of his chair, and the pop wasn't even all that loud. Maybe he was scared of balloons. Maybe *that* was why he was taking Balloon Day off. It was funny to think of a grizzled old guy like Wally being afraid of balloons, but people are afraid of all kinds of things. I once saw a neighbor shriek and run inside after seeing a caterpillar, and he was a grown man! Even Dylan had just told me he was afraid of the dark.

I was only scared of one thing, and it wasn't silly at all—I was afraid of that coffeemaker.

y dad had over a thousand books, about everything from bread mold to black holes. I figured he had to have one about making coffee.

Dad saw me going through the shelves. "Looking for something to read?" He sounded hopeful.

"I need a book about coffee. I need to know how to make it."

"Your mother already made some. Anyway, you're too young to drink coffee."

"Drink it? *Bleah!*" Coffee was just a mud

puddle in a cup. For some reason, adults hadn't figured that out. "I need to make coffee next week at work."

"Oh. Well, watch me make it tomorrow morning."

"We have the wrong kind of machine." Ours didn't shimmy or shake or make whistling noises. It just gurgled a bit and dripped glop into a glass pot.

"OK. Then read the instructions that came with the coffeemaker."

"I don't know if we still have them." The Pines' machine was so old, the original instructions probably came carved in stone.

"I'm sure you'll be fine." Dad left the room whistling. He probably didn't mean to sound like the coffee machine at work, but he did.

I looked at his books for a while. Dad is interested in *everything*. He has books about history, science, cooking, business, and entertainment. I saw a book about balloons and took it off the shelf. If he had a book about making balloon animals, I could have taught Abby a thing or two. But it wasn't about that kind of balloon. It was about the kind of balloon you ride in. That book was kind of interesting. It made me want to ride in a hot-air balloon.

• • •

I was bored all week. I didn't have school, and I didn't have a job. I called some of my friends, but it seemed like everybody was either at camp or on vacation with their family.

I wasn't just bored. I missed the Porcupines. They'd gone on road trips before, but this one felt longer. It was because they were playing so well and were almost in first place. It made every game more important. I wished like anything I could be there. I missed listening to the guys crack jokes in the locker room. I missed shagging fly balls during batting practice. I missed high-fiving the players when they scored a run. I missed being part of the team.

I missed baseball so much that I volunteered to be a batboy for a T-ball tournament at the park. But they wouldn't take me. The woman in charge said I was too old to play and too young to volunteer.

"But I'm a professional!" I showed her my Porcupines badge.

"That's nice," she said. "But there are rules. Why don't you stay and cheer for the players? They can always use some encouragement."

So I watched part of the tournament. It just made me miss the Porcupines even more.

I also spent a lot of time playing with my baseball cards. I'm always trying to figure out the best way to sort them. Should I organize the binders by year or by team? And inside each binder, should I sort the players by card number, by name, by position, or by uniform number?

The toughest decision was figuring out which cards should go into my red binder. The red binder is my baseball card hall of fame. The cards in there are not always the rarest cards or the most famous players. They're simply my favorite cards.

Some of the Porcupines think those cards are magic. Earlier in the season, a Rafael Furcal card helped Mike Stammer, the shortstop, turn an unassisted triple play. Later, a Bengie Molina card helped Sammy Solaris, the designated hitter, steal the first base of his career. I didn't think those cards were magic, but I *did* think they helped remind players what they were capable of.

• • •

Meanwhile, the Porcupines won five out of six games that week, with one day off. When they came home, they were tied for first place with the Rosedale Rogues. Usually at this time of year, the Porcupines were just trying not to wind up in last place. This season, it seemed like anything was possible.

I got to work early on Friday, like Wally had asked. The coffee was already brewing in the kitchen area. The machine shivered and gasped a cloud of steam.

"I wanted to see you make the coffee so I can do it tomorrow," I told Wally.

"Sorry. I didn't think about that."

"Did the machine come with instructions?" I asked, remembering what Dad had suggested.

"Oh, those are long gone," Wally replied. "But don't worry. I'll write up what to do."

Wayne Zane overheard us.

"You want to make coffee like Wally's?" the Pines' catcher asked me. "First, you need some old ground-up baseball mitts. Throw about six gloves into the pot, fill it with hot water, boil it for a few hours, and you're done."

"Use twice as many mitts and be sure to throw in some pine tar," added the pitcher, Lance Pantaño. "Wally's coffee is too weak."

"If you guys don't like my coffee, you don't have to drink it," Wally said as he filled his own mug with the steaming black brew.

"Just sayin'," said Wayne.

"The coffee is fine," said Myung Young, the center fielder. He filled his mug, poured in lots of creamer, and dumped in three or four packets of sugar.

"That's not coffee," said Wayne. "That's a milk shake."

"It's too hot to be a milk shake," said Myung.

Lance filled his Porcupines mug. There was a piece of tape on the mug that said "Property of Lance."

Wayne was right behind him. I guessed Wally's coffee couldn't have been *that* bad.

• • •

I followed Wally around. He had a checklist with everything from "Put out fresh towels" to "Count shoelaces in the supply chest" on it.

"Nothing you need to do is a big deal," he told me. "It's a million little deals."

"Got it."

Dylan came in, nodded hello, and started changing.

"How was Otter Lake? Guess you weren't eaten by a bear," I said.

"Nope," Dylan answered. He scratched his arm. "I got eaten by one hundred thousand mosquitoes, though. Are you ready to be in charge tomorrow?"

"I'm not in charge," I said. "Just twice as busy."

Wally was still going through his checklist. I followed him to the Pines' equipment room. He flipped the switch. The lightbulb flickered and went out.

"Uh-oh," Wally said. "We have to find the flashlight."

"Where is it?"

"In here somewhere." He groped around on a shelf—I could hear things getting tipped over and knocked around.

"I can find it," I told him.

"Thanks. And good luck." Wally propped the door open so I had some light from the hall. I searched the shadowy shelves until I found the flashlight. It was as long as my forearm. I turned it on. It shone like a spotlight.

I found Dylan so I could show it to him.

"This is what you need for your next camping trip. You could spot a bear a mile off with it."

"So I can blind him?" Dylan held up his hand to block the beam. I'd forgotten to turn off the flashlight.

"So you won't have to be afraid of the dark," I explained.

"*Shh!*" Dylan said. "I don't need all these guys to hear. Besides, I'm not afraid of the dark. I'm afraid of being eaten by bears."

"Can I borrow that flashlight?" asked Sammy. He took the flashlight from me and pretended to shine the beam through his hand. "I tweaked my left hand, and I've been meaning to get it X-rayed."

Wayne peeked over his shoulder. "Looks like a misassociated linguini hypotenuse." He put a hand on Sammy's elbow. "You'll need surgery, Sammy."

"Will I be able to play the banjo after the operation?"

"If things go well," said Wayne in a somber voice.

"Awesome," said Sammy. "I've always wanted to play the banjo."

"Knock it off," said Wally. He reached for the flashlight, but Sammy handed it off to Tommy Harris, the third baseman.

Tommy backed up and held it in front of him like a lightsaber. He made *zwip* and *zwoop* sounds.

"Use the force, Tommy!" Wayne said helpfully.

"Might as well be teaching kindergarten," Wally grumbled.

Tommy handed the flashlight over to the

manager. "You seem a little tense, Wally. What's up?"

"I got a lot on my mind."

"He doesn't like balloons," I explained. "Tomorrow's Balloon Day, and Wally . . ." I saw Wally staring at me and stopped.

"Is that true, Wally?" asked Tommy. "You have a problem with balloons?"

Wally turned red. "Mind your own business," he said. "I got to go change a lightbulb." He stalked off with the flashlight.

"You don't even need that flashlight," Wayne shouted after him. "Your face is glowing like a lantern."

Dylan nudged me. "Maybe you shouldn't have said anything."

"Oops." I went after Wally.

He was unfolding a stepladder so he could change that lightbulb in the equipment room.

"Sorry," I said. "I didn't mean to say anything."

"What's done is done," he said. "Here, hold the flashlight for me."

I pointed the flashlight while Wally clambered up the ladder. He reached up, unscrewed the knob, and took off the glass fixture.

POP! A balloon burst behind us.

Wally dropped the glass fixture, which bounced off the ladder and smashed against the floor.

The equipment room door was still propped open. I saw Wayne Zane zipping back into the locker room. I think he was laughing.

Wally muttered something under his breath. He changed the bulb while I swept up the broken glass. Then we went back to the locker room. Several of the players were snickering.

"I'd better go take batting practice," said Wayne. "I don't want to *pop* it up today."

"Hey, maybe you'll *blast* a homer," said Tommy.

"You could *bust* the game wide open," added the DH, Sammy Solaris.

"I just hope I don't *blow* a save," said Ryan Kimball, the closer.

"You guys are about as funny as a rain delay," said Wally.

"Hey, Wally, don't go off . . . ," Teddy Larrabee started.

". . . mad?" Wayne finished his sentence.

"Hey, that was my line," said Teddy.

It was my turn to help the visiting team, the West Valley Varmints. The Varmints were the worst team in the league this season. They looked pretty gloomy on the bench, hanging their heads and barely talking to each other. The Porcupines were always kidding around, even when they were losing. No matter how the game went, the Pines always had fun. The Varmints weren't having fun.

The Varmints started off not hitting well. Ernie Hecker had a lot of fun shouting insults at them. Ernie has the loudest mouth in all of

Pine City. He always sits above the visitors' dugout so he can let the visiting team have it.

"Hey, why did you even bring a bat?" he yelled at a player who struck out looking at a called third strike. An inning later a batter swung wildly at three pitches, missing every one. "Aim for the ball next time!" Ernie shouted helpfully. In the ninth inning the Varmints finally scored a run, but they were down by ten runs, so it didn't help. "Whatever!" Ernie shouted.

I almost felt sorry for the Varmints, but I saw on the scoreboard that the Rosedale Rogues had won their game. The Porcupines needed the win to stay tied for first place. Lucky for them, they had three more games against the Varmints.

• • •

Only a couple of players were left in the

Porcupines' locker room by the time I got over there.

"That was a real blowout!" Wayne Zane told me. "I've seen some blowouts, but, man, that was a blowout."

"Yeah, yeah, yeah," said Wally. "I heard you the first time you made that joke."

"Just sayin'," said Wayne.

There was a lion in my locker this time. It was made of twisted yellow balloons, with an orange balloon for a mane. I realized it would be the last balloon animal, since tomorrow was the big day.

"What did you get?" I asked Dylan.

"Another one of these, whatever it is." He held up a tangled mess of red, green, and white balloons.

"Maybe it's Santa Claus climbing a Christmas tree?" I said.

"Or being eaten by one," said Dylan.

"Don't forget to get here extra-early tomorrow," Wally told me. "I'll leave my checklist in your locker."

"Will do," I answered.

"Hey, Wally," said Wayne. "Are you taking the whole day off just because you don't like balloons?"

"Don't be silly," said Wally. "Something came up."

"Like a helium balloon?" Sammy asked.

"You can level with us, Wally. We'll understand." Wayne gave him a serious look. "Are you afraid of Balloon Day?"

"I'm avoiding the windbags," said Wally. "Not having to deal with the balloons is a bonus."

• • •

When I got home, I put the lion on my

dresser next to the giraffe, the crocodile, and the monkey. I had almost enough animals for a balloon safari park. Abby was still giving me only jungle animals. I liked them a lot, but I wondered what she was up to.

I thought again about the many things I had to do with Wally away. Just thinking about making the coffee made my stomach flip. What if I messed up? Lance Pantaño needed coffee to pitch. That was his ritual. If he didn't get it, he might not pitch well. And if he didn't pitch

well, the Porcupines would lose. And if the Porcupines lost, they might lose ground to the Rosedale Rogues.

It was a lot to have hanging over my head.

I glanced at the shelf with my baseball cards. Magic or not, maybe they could help.

The card I needed wasn't in the red binder. I went to the binder where I keep all of the cards for mascots, umpires, managers, and announcers—anybody who isn't an actual player. The baseball card companies sometimes print cards for other people who have made their name in the game. I didn't have any cards for clubhouse managers, let alone batboys, but there were plenty of manager cards to choose from. I decided on Joe Torre. He'd won a lot of World Series rings, after all. I hoped he also knew how to make coffee.

I was the only one in the Porcupines' locker room. I'd gotten there super-early, before any of the players or coaches. I looked through my notes from Wally. "Make coffee" was on the checklist. He didn't give me any further instructions.

"You can do this," I told myself.

The coffee machine was on top of a little table. Next to it was a small fridge with a microwave on top. That was "the kitchen area," as the guys called it. The table had a drawer, but there was nothing in it except packets of creamer and sugar and some stir sticks.

I opened the coffee machine. There was a metal basket inside atop a rod that poked up from the middle. I didn't know how any of it worked, but it looked like you filled the main part with water and the basket part with coffee.

How hard could it be?

I lugged the machine across the locker room to the sink and turned on the water. When it hit the line on the inside that said "Full," I turned it off. So far, so good.

The coffee machine was a lot heavier to lug back. When I set it down, I opened the can of coffee and scooped it in until the basket was full. I remembered what Lance said about making the coffee stronger—I'd surprise him with extra-strong coffee. I piled more coffee in the basket until there was a little mound on top.

Then I slowly screwed the basket on top of the rod, put the lid on, plugged in the machine, and threw the switch.

A little light above the tap turned red. A minute later the coffee machine started to gurgle. There, that wasn't so hard.

"Thanks, Joe," I said, patting my pocket where the Joe Torre card was. Still, maybe now was a good time to do things way on the *other* side of the room. I felt better with a wall of lockers between the coffee machine and me.

I spent a half hour putting clean uniforms in the right lockers. When I put Lance Pantaño's uniform away, I noticed his mug with the "Property of Lance" label. The mug was brown as tar inside. I took it over to the sink and scrubbed it for him and then put it back where I had found it. His extra-strong coffee would taste even better out of a clean mug.

The coffee machine was whistling and rattling, but no louder than usual. I took a quick look. It was puffing steam, but it always did that.

"Piece of cake, Joe," I said, grinning.

"Who are you talking to?" It was Lance. He was the first player to show up.

"Er . . . nobody," I said. Baseball players have all kinds of superstitions and rituals, but even they would think I was crazy for talking to a baseball card.

"Oh, good, you're making coffee." Lance grabbed his mug from his locker. "Hey, who washed my mug?"

"I did."

"I never wash it! It's bad luck." Lance looked sadly at the mug.

"I'm sorry. I didn't know! I noticed it was dirty, and . . ."

SHRIEEEK!

Both of us nearly hit the ceiling.

SHRIEEEK! SHRIEEEK! SHRIEEEK!

That noise wasn't human, or even animal. It was the whistling of the coffeemaker—only it was a hundred times louder than usual!

"What did you do?!" Lance shouted.

"I just filled the basket with coffee!" I shouted back. "I didn't do anything weird!"

"Wally only fills the basket halfway!" said Lance.

I had filled the basket all the way *and* rounded off the top. This was officially a coffee disaster.

Clang-clang-clang-clang-clang!

"Uh-oh." I peered around the lockers at the coffeemaker. Steam was blasting out from under the lid. The whole machine was shaking and rattling right toward the edge of the table.

"I got this!" said Lance. He came over, wearing Wayne Zane's catcher's mask and chest protector. "Here," he said, handing me the fire extinguisher. "Just in case."

He got to the coffee machine just before it shook itself off the table. The machine shrieked again. It let loose a cloud of steam. Some black goop oozed out of the lid and dribbled down the side. I smelled fresh tar and burning rubber.

"Maybe you should just unplug it!" I hollered. Lance reached for the cord.

Suddenly, the light on the machine went from red to orange and the shrieking stopped. There was one more gasp of brown steam, and the machine stopped rattling.

Wayne Zane came in, with Teddy right behind him. Wayne looked at the pitcher wearing his catcher's gear.

"I forgot today was opposite day," said

Wayne. He saw me with the extinguisher. "If I see a fire, I'll let you know."

"Chad made coffee," Lance explained.

"Of course," said Wayne. "It all makes sense now." He went to his locker and grabbed his mug. "I hope you remembered to throw in an extra baseball mitt." The catcher turned the spigot on the coffee machine. A thick brown liquid gurgled out.

"Whoa! It looks like you threw in an extra glove and a few ground-up bats." Wayne sniffed the coffee and took a sip. "Wow, that's strong coffee."

"Let me try it," said Teddy. He grabbed the cup, blew on it, and took a sip himself. His eyes widened. "I think I'll need help blinking for the next few hours."

"Might as well try it too," said Lance. He took off the catcher's gear and returned with his mug.

"Is your mug *clean*?" asked Wayne.

"Yeah, it's bad luck," Lance replied. "But if anything will crud it up again quick, it's this stuff." He pulled the tap and filled the mug. "Mmm . . . smells good," he said.

He took a big gulp.

"Chad," said Lance.

"Yeah?"

"This is the best cup of coffee I've had since I left Puerto Rico. It's perfect."

6

The Pines headed out for batting practice. Dylan and I followed to field fly balls.

"Hey, check that out," I called to him. A great big balloon—not a toy balloon but an actual hot-air balloon—floated just above the outfield wall. It was a promotion by the local radio station. The hot-air balloon was only half-full now, but by game time it would be high up in the sky. Six lucky fans would be up there watching the game.

"That would be fun," said Dylan.

"Yeah." I would have been calling in like crazy to win a ticket, but ballpark employees weren't allowed to enter. Anyway, I had to work down here on the field.

Spike, the junior mascot, was over by third base, waving at the fans as they came into the ballpark.

"Hi, Spike! Thanks for all the balloon animals!" Dylan said as we passed.

Spike just nodded. Mascots aren't supposed to talk.

"So what are those crazy things you gave Dylan supposed to be?" I asked. "Are they spiders? I guessed spiders because of that time . . ." I stopped, realizing that Spike's head was drooping. The mascot was embarrassed.

Spike reached back and ran a hand over the quills on the costume.

"Oh! They're balloon *porcupines!*" I said.

"Of course they're porcupines," Dylan said. "They're great, Spike."

The junior mascot perked up, high-fived Dylan, and headed off to wave at the fans in deep right field.

"I think you hurt Abby's feelings," said Dylan.

"I didn't mean to." I vowed to keep my yap shut for the rest of the day.

• • •

Teddy Larrabee was the first one to take his practice swings. "The Bear" sent a ball almost all the way to the fence. I chased after it and caught it, nearly crashing into Myung Young, the center fielder. He liked to practice his fielding during batting practice. Myung was a great fielder and fun to watch. This time he'd been running backwards and nearly ran over me.

"You should have called that," said Myung.

"Sorry." I changed my promise to myself. I would keep my yap shut unless I was running down a fly ball.

• • •

I walked by the bull pen after batting practice. Lance was warming up.

"Ouch!" Zeke said, tossing the ball back. He was the pitching coach and doubled as bull-pen catcher. "You've got some real heat today, Lance."

"I feel great," said Lance. He said something else in Spanish. Zeke also spoke Spanish. His full name was Ezequiel Olivarra, and he was from the Dominican Republic. I wish I knew Spanish, because then I would understand what they were saying.

Zeke must have read my mind. "Lance told me to try your coffee. He said it's the best he's had since he came to the mainland."

"Thanks!" I had to talk when I had to be polite.

Dylan tugged on the sleeve of my jersey.

"There's a guy who wants to talk to you. Over there." He pointed his thumb toward the visitors' dugout. "He asked me to come get you."

"Who?"

"Some guy in the stands. He says he knows you."

"Um. . . . OK." I hoped it wasn't Ernie Hecker. Why would Ernie want to talk to me? I wondered. I'd only met him once. For that matter, why would he need Dylan to come get me? He could have just shouted at me from across the field. I would have heard him.

I went around the diamond, behind the backstop, since the Varmints were still warming up in the infield. I noticed the hot-air balloon was now way up there. The wind pulled it toward right field. I could see little people-shaped blobs in the basket, looking down. I hoped the fans up there had brought binoculars so they could tell the teams apart.

I saw a hand waving frantically at me from above the visitors' dugout. I got a little closer and saw who it belonged to—Uncle Rick!

Uncle Rick was the biggest baseball fan in the world. He taught me everything I know . . . or at least everything I knew until I got this job.

"Hey, Chad!" Uncle Rick called. He came down the steps and leaned over the railing. "I finally cashed in that rain check!"

"Cool!"

Uncle Rick had tried to see a Pines' game earlier in the season, but it was rained out.

"The thing is, they were all out of tickets," he said. "I told them that I had come all the

way from the city, and they said, sorry, we don't have a single seat left. Can you believe it? Anyway, this guy overheard me and told me he had an extra ticket, so it all worked out. Great seats, too! I met a big fan!" Uncle Rick pointed at his seat. The guy sitting in the next seat was Ernie Hecker!

"Great!" I said. "Did you happen to bring ear plugs?"

"Huh? Why would I do that?"

"No reason."

"Hey, Ernie!" Uncle Rick shouted. He took out his cell phone and waved at Ernie to come down. "You need to take a picture of me with my nephew. He's in professional baseball! Hey, too bad you're not working in the Varmints' dugout. I could talk to you more during the game."

"I would swap with Dylan, but I'm acting

clubhouse manager today," I told my uncle. Wally never said that exactly, but it was mostly true and it sounded really important.

"My nephew!" Uncle Rick boasted, pointing me out to anyone in the stands who could see me. "Acting clubhouse manager! Right there!" He could have won a loudness competition with Ernie Hecker.

he Varmints made three quick outs in the top of the first inning. The Porcupines came out swinging and scored three runs. After that, I was busy and was only half paying attention. With Wally gone, there was a lot more to do. I had to find Sammy some new batting gloves because the strap broke on one of his. Wayne had a sore hand and needed ointment. Grumps—that's what everyone called the Porcupines' manager—needed new lead for his mechanical pencil. It took me forever to find it.

It seemed like every time I finished one errand, I had to run and get something else, or chase after a foul ball, or fetch a bat. I lost track of the game, which is how I got into trouble.

In the bottom of the fifth inning, Lance handed me his "Property of Lance" mug. He gave me a little nod, but he didn't say a word. I guessed that he wanted more coffee. I'd already refilled the mug a couple of times. I went and topped it off and brought it back. I hoped the coffee hadn't gotten cold. He took it, sipped, and smiled.

"Still perfect?" I asked.

He looked at me with wide eyes and nearly dropped the mug.

I glanced sideways and saw that everyone in the dugout was staring at me.

I checked my zipper. Nothing wrong there.

I took off my cap to see if there was gum

on it. It was fine. I looked back at the Pines'
dugout.

"What?" I asked.

Lance shook his head at me.

Teddy came over and took me by the
shoulder.

"Over here," he said. He led me to the other
end of the dugout.

Grumps was watching me with wide,
bloodshot eyes. He was snorting and fuming,
and his head looked like a balloon, swelling and
swelling. I though it might pop.

"It's OK, Grumps," Teddy whispered. "I'll
talk to the boy." He waved at me to stand right
at the entrance to the field, and then he pointed
across the field at the scoreboard. It didn't just
show how many runs had been scored, it also
showed the hits and errors each team had.

The Varmints had zero hits.

The Porcupines had zero errors.

I couldn't talk at first. I forced the words out, sounding as small and squeaky as a leaky balloon. Or maybe I just had balloons on the brain. "Are there . . . " I asked. "Does Lance have any . . ."

"No, he doesn't have any walks," Teddy replied. "No hit batsmen. No errors. No hits. No nothing."

"So the Varmints . . ."

"That's right. The Varmints have not had a base runner through five innings," the Bear whispered. "Fifteen up, fifteen down."

"It's a p—" I started.

"Don't say it again!" said Teddy.

"Don't make things worse." He glanced at the other end of the dugout. Lance sipped from the mug of coffee in his left hand. His right arm—his pitching arm—was wrapped up in a warm towel to keep the muscles loose.

I wanted to cry. I couldn't breathe. I plopped down, nearly landing in Grumps's lap. Grumps nudged me out of the way so he could see what was happening on the field. He shot me a look that was worse than if he had yelled at me for two straight hours.

I finally inhaled. I didn't say it, but I thought it: Lance was more than halfway to . . . *a perfect game*. A perfect game was when a pitcher didn't let a single player reach base in the entire game: no hits, no walks, no errors, no nothing. Only twenty pitchers had ever done that in all of major league history. I didn't know how many perfect games there had been in Single-A minor league baseball. But I did know this: there had never been one in our Prairie League!

A perfect game in any league is practically impossible, even against a team in a slump. Even five straight perfect innings is something. On the sports channel, they break into other games if a pitcher has a perfect game going through five innings. It's a really big deal.

I looked at the hot-air balloon floating over the right field wall. I suddenly wished I were in it, so I could untie the line and float far, far away and never be seen again in Pine City Park. Because besides knowing how amazing and rare perfect games are, I knew two other things.

One: you never, *ever*, talk about a perfect game when it's in progress. You don't say anything like "Wow, it's a perfect game so far!" You just watch the game quietly or you jinx it.

Two: you don't talk to the pitcher when he's having a great game. You just leave him alone.

I had broken both rules in two seconds. It didn't even matter that I wasn't talking about the game. I'd blabbed Wally's secrets lately and also hurt Abby's feelings, but this was the worst mess my mouth had gotten me into yet. I might have ruined Lance Pantaño's chance at making history!

• • •

The Porcupines now had five runs, but no amount of runs would make me feel better if Lance didn't stay perfect. I think the whole team felt the same way.

It was the quietest the Pines' dugout had ever been. Nobody talked to anybody else. Even Wayne Zane took his bat without cracking a single joke. He went up to the plate and hit a fly ball to right field, came back, and handed me the bat without a word. I expected him to say that the hot-air balloon got in his eyes or that he was afraid of hitting the ball too hard and knocking the balloon down, but he just muttered a thank-you and told me to bring him his catcher's gear. Teddy Larrabee batted next, and he was the same way. The Bear usually tugs my hat brim down over my eyes, but this time he didn't. He just took his bat and went to the plate.

Teddy grounded out to first, and the inning was over. I passed Lance as I was taking Teddy's bat to the rack. He stood up, unwrapped the towel from his arm, handed it to me, and headed for the mound. His shoulders slumped, and he moved slowly, like a man walking to his own doom.

The perfect game was about to end—and it was all my fault.

Lance's first pitch in the top of the sixth inning nearly ended everything. The Varmints' batter swung and connected, sending the ball high and deep to center field. The crowd groaned. It looked like the perfect game, the no-hitter, and the shutout were all about to fly over the fence with that ball.

But Myung Young saved the day, running practically straight up the fence to snag the ball just before it sailed out of the park for a home run. The crowd sighed in relief, then cheered. Lance pointed at Myung to show how much he appreciated the catch.

Pantaño struck the next batter out on three pitches, but the third pitch glanced off Wayne's glove and rolled away. The batter took off. There's this crazy rule that if the catcher drops the third strike, the batter can try to reach first base before the ball gets there. Wayne scrambled after the ball, picked it up, and made a sideways throw from his knees. The ball reached Teddy at first base just in time to get the runner out.

The crowd cheered again.

The perfect game was still intact.

The third batter hammered the ball into the grass. It bounced way, way, way into the air, over the pitcher's head. That's called a *chopper*, and it's kind of a lousy trick, especially when you're using it to break up a perfect game.

Mike Stammer leaped into the air. It looked like Mike didn't even catch the ball before throwing it. It looked like he just swatted the ball over to first base, using the scoop of his glove like a lacrosse stick. The ball got to Teddy Larrabee—but was it there in time?

The umpire squinted and made sure Teddy had the ball. He looked at the first base bag and mulled it over. Finally, he gave the sign: thumb over the shoulder. *Out!*

The Varmints' batter shook his head in disbelief while the crowd went crazy.

Lance came back to the dugout, sat down at the far end, away from everyone else, and hung his head. Zeke, the pitching coach, rewrapped Lance's arm, but they didn't say one word to each other. You'd never know Lance had just pitched another perfect inning. He looked like someone who'd given up thirty-seven runs. He'd only gotten through the inning because of three great plays. He hadn't pitched that well.

The Porcupines' dugout was still tense, and that made everyone crabby. Danny O'Brien batted first and scolded me for bringing him Brian Daniels's bat by mistake. A couple of batters later, George Lincoln, the second baseman, muttered something at the umpire. Grumps had to go out there and calm "the President" down before he got thrown out of the game. Tommy Harris, who was almost always smiling, wasn't smiling. He took a couple of swings in the on-deck circle, but he didn't get a chance to bat because George was rung up on strikes for the third out.

Lance stood up and shook his head. He dropped the towel and headed back to the mound. His knees looked wobbly. But he needed only nine more outs, I realized.

The first batter took five straight pitches before he swung the bat. The next pitch was

probably out of the strike zone. It would have meant a walk, and the end to the perfect game, but the batter swung at it and missed. Lance got lucky again.

The next batter hit a line drive to right field. Danny had to really hurry. He caught the ball, and the crowd cheered. His catch wasn't as good as Myung Young's catch from the last inning, but it was still a really good catch. And it was another out.

Two down, seven to go.

The third batter had an average of over .350. Of all the Varmint batters, he scared me the most.

Lance asked for a time-out to catch his breath. The brief pause felt like forever, but I didn't want it to end. Everything right now was still perfect. One pitch from now, it might not be.

Lance asked for a new ball, got it, and threw

a fastball. The batter swung and hit the ball hard, sending it to deep right field. It looked like a goner, and it would have been, but the wind carried it into the seats. Foul ball! I looked up and saw the little shadows in the balloon basket jumping up and down.

The batter swung at the next pitch and bounced the ball back to Lance. He threw to first and headed for the dugout. "Saved by the wind," he muttered as he took his spot on the bench. "But I can't count on the wind every time."

The fans burst into "Take Me Out to the Ball Game." I'd forgotten it was the seventh inning stretch. I heard Ernie Hecker's tuneless booming over the rest of the crowd, and then a second voice, way out of key with the first, booming just as loudly: Uncle Rick.

Uncle Rick! He'd only had one chance in his whole life to see a no-hitter, and he missed that game because of me—he had to leave in the middle of the game because I was being born. If Lance stayed perfect, then Uncle Rick would finally get another chance to see a whole no-hitter from start to finish. A perfect game *is* a no-hitter, only better.

When I sat down, I felt something in my pocket. I took it out and looked at it. It was the Joe Torre card. Fat lot of good it had done me, since Joe Torre knew better than to jinx a pitcher's perfect game. Joe looked back at me. His face was grim and seemed to say: "Chad, do something."

I owed it to Lance to fix this, and I owed it to my uncle.

The way to fix it was right there in my hand too. I needed a card, and it had to be one from the red binder. The question was, which card? I had cards for four perfect game pitchers in my red binder: Roy Halladay, Randy Johnson, Mark Buehrle, and Dallas Braden. Which one should I give to Lance? Did it matter? Perfect was perfect; there was no way for one to be more perfect than another. Did any of those pitchers have a batboy try to ruin it for them?

Uncle Rick would know! He knew more about baseball than anyone. I just needed to get over there and explain things to him.

But there were three problems.

One: The Porcupines would be coming up to bat any minute. I was needed here.

Two: Even if I got away and talked to Uncle Rick, my red binder was at home, not here at the ballpark.

Three: The hot-air balloon was crashing down onto the playing field over in right field.

The hot-air balloon didn't pop and fly around the way that toy balloons do. It just drifted down until the basket bounced on the ground. Then it rose a few feet and dropped again. It all happened softly and slowly, so I didn't think anybody in the basket was hurt. It actually looked like fun. A crashing hot-air balloon could be an awesome carnival ride.

The next time the balloon touched the ground, it tipped over sideways. The Varmints' right fielder raced to get out of its path. Too

late! He was swallowed up by yards of balloon cloth. Security guards and staff ran to help. The crowd was buzzing. Victor Snapp, the announcer, told everyone to be calm. Several people held the basket steady and helped the passengers climb out. Two other guards helped the right fielder burrow out from under the cloth. The balloon rose up again, lifting and dragging all its parts. It headed toward the seats. People in the front rows scurried out of the way.

I glanced up and down the Pines' dugout. Everybody was watching the balloon with open mouths and wide eyes. Everybody, that is, except Lance Pantaño. He stared down at his shoes. He didn't even seem to notice what was going on.

This was my big chance! I hurried out of the dugout. A guard stopped me. He thought I was heading to the hot-air balloon.

"Thanks, kid, but we have all the help we need. Better stay away."

"All right," I told him. I went the long way around instead. I passed through the locker room and circled the concourse. It was deserted. People were glued to their seats, watching the slow-speed balloon crash.

I tried to make my way to Uncle Rick, but so many people were standing on the steps that I couldn't get through. So I went to the visitors' dugout to find Dylan. The Varmints were crowded around the right fielder, who'd been helped off the field. He seemed to be shaken up but OK.

"It just kept coming after me," he said. "It was like this horror movie I saw once about a giant blob—only this blob could fly."

Dylan was kneeling, listening along with everyone else.

"*Psst*. Dylan."

"Huh?" He looked back, saw me, and came over. "What's up?"

"I need you to help me save Lance Pantaño's—" I nearly jinxed it again, right then, but I stopped myself. "I need a baseball card from home, but I don't know which one."

"I can't leave!" Dylan said. "I'm working. Besides, I don't know anything about baseball cards."

"I know, but my uncle Rick does. He's the guy who talked to you earlier. He's sitting next to Ernie." I explained as best I could—Uncle Rick would know the perfect card to choose, and he had a cell phone, so he could call my dad and tell him to bring it.

"How will your dad get in?" asked Dylan. "The game is sold out."

"Ugh!" It was just one problem after another.

As ballpark staff, we could ask for guest passes, but we had to ask for them in advance. "Tell my uncle Rick to tell my dad to tell the guys at the gate that he's a hot-air balloon expert," I said.

It took a second for Dylan to make sense of that sentence. "*Is* your dad a hot-air balloon expert?" he asked.

"He has a book about balloons. He can just tuck it under his arm and carry a toolbox."

"I don't think it'll work, Chad."

"It doesn't hurt to try," I said. Could it? Could Dad be arrested for impersonating a hot-air balloon repairman? "We need to do something, Dylan, or else . . . Well, I can't say what else."

"Does this have something to do with Lance's perfect game?"

"*Gabbagah!*" I shouted.

"What?"

"You *never* talk about a perfect game while it's in progress," I told him. "But . . . wait, do you even know what a perfect game is?"

"It's one where the pitcher doesn't let anyone get on base," Dylan explained. "Lance hasn't so far today. He got lucky a few times, especially when the wind blew that home run ball into foul territory. There was also Myung's catch, and some other great plays on defense, and the Varmints swung at some bad pitches. But none of that matters. Perfect is perfect."

"This means that you do know something about the game, *and* that you've been paying attention. You care! That means you're a fan, Dylan!"

"I guess so," he admitted.

"But you must not jinx a perfect game," I told him. "That's serious, Dylan. Never do it." I didn't tell him I'd nearly done the same thing.

In fact, we might be doing it right now. We had just said "perfect" six times.

"Sorry," Dylan said.

"It's OK. You can help me fix it. I need to convince Lance that he isn't jinxed. My uncle will know which baseball card can do that. My dad can put the card in the red binder and tell the guy at the gate he's an emergency hot-air balloon repairman. That's why I need you to talk to Uncle Rick."

"I'm on it," he said. "Wait—why does the card need to be in the red binder?"

"Because that's what makes the cards magic." I started back for the Porcupines' dugout.

10

Lance was fidgeting, jiggling his leg, and drumming his fingers on the bench. "I just want to get back out there," he said to Zeke. "I want to pitch."

"It won't be much longer," the pitching coach promised him.

Some of the guards and the field crew had pulled the balloon out of the seats and into the middle of the field. Now it was a game of tug-of-war, as the wind kept pulling on the partly inflated balloon. One of the men working on the balloon looked kind of like Wally. I shook my head.

The guy was pretty far away, but he sure looked like Wally.

He looked even more like Wally when he stood up and walked over to the dugout.

"Everyone's OK," Wally said. "But it'll be a while before we get that thing off the field."

"Aren't you supposed to be on vacation?" asked Sammy.

"Is this how you spend your vacation?" Wayne asked. "Going to baseball games?"

"Sometimes," said Wally, "but not today. I was up in that balloon. I'm the pilot."

We all stared at him. Nobody said a word.

Wally was a hot-air balloon pilot?

"Well, they couldn't find anyone else to fly it," said Wally. "Somebody found out I had a hot-air-balloon pilot's license, and one thing led to another."

"How long have you had a balloon pilot's license?" Sammy asked.

"Thirty-odd years," said Wally. "I do have a life outside of the locker room, you know."

"But I thought you were scared of balloons," I said. "You were jumping every time a balloon popped."

"Hmm," said Wally. "I get a little edgy just before a flight. When a toy balloon pops, it reminds me what might happen. But once I'm in the basket, I feel fine."

"I'm the same way before a game," said Tommy.

"Me too," said Teddy.

Several other players nodded in agreement.

"Wally, can I ride with you sometime?" Sammy asked. "I've always wanted to go up in a hot-air balloon."

"I think you're going to need a bigger balloon," Wayne told Wally. He patted Sammy's big stomach.

"Hey!" said Sammy.

"I'll get a bigger balloon, but the burner will never blow enough hot air to keep it up," said Wally. "So, Wayne, you're coming too."

All the guys laughed.

"Just sayin'," said Wally, heading into the locker room.

Before Wayne could get another word in, my dad showed up. It wasn't hard to recognize him: he was wearing a fake-looking nose and funny glasses with big eyebrows. They were left over from a Halloween party we had a few years ago.

"Hello. I'm with Lighter-Than-Air Vehicle Refurbishment and Repair," he announced. "I heard there was a situation? Aha, there it is. I'll go right over. Young man, please follow me." Dad shoved his toolbox at me, and I took it. He trotted purposefully onto the field, and I hustled after him.

"Dad, this is ridiculous."

"I've been to the locker room before," he reminded me. "I had to disguise myself. By the way, I've got your cards."

We got to the "situation." Dad introduced himself and then eyed the balloon and clucked a couple of times. "Looks like a breach in one of the gore panels," he said. "What do you want to do, repair the breach and re-inflate? Or exhaust the balloon and pack it up?"

I didn't know if any of that was real balloon talk, but it sure sounded right.

"We just want to get on with the game," said the head groundskeeper. "What's quicker?"

Dad peered up at the top of the balloon. "It looks like the deflation port is still sealed. Why isn't it vented?"

"The cord snapped," somebody explained. "That's why the pilot had to make a crash landing. He had to shut off the burner so the balloon wouldn't burst."

"Hmm. Well, if we wait long enough, the balloon will eventually deflate. But if you're in a hurry, I need to get to the deflation port or cut the envelope." Dad made a little whistling noise. "She's a beaut, so it would be a shame to cut 'er up."

The *envelope*? Dad sure sounded like he knew his stuff. While they were talking, I cracked open his toolbox. The red binder was wedged inside at an angle.

"Young man," said Dad.

"Yeah?" I shut the lid on the box.

"Hold my glasses." He took them off—the fake nose came too—and handed them to me. The crew members looked at each other, but nobody said a word.

Dad leaped up and grabbed handfuls of loose balloon fabric. I thought he was trying to pull it down. But he was climbing up! He scaled the balloon until he was able to get his fingers into a crease at the top.

Suddenly, there was a loud ripping noise as Dad opened a flap lined with Velcro. The balloon let out a big sigh. Dad plunged, but he grabbed on to the side of the balloon before his feet hit the ground. He let go and dropped the last few inches.

"That'll do 'er." Dad put his fake glasses back on.

The crew spread the balloon and pressed out the air. Then they rolled it up and stuffed it in the basket. It took six people to carry the balloon basket off the field. The crowd clapped.

"The game will resume in just a few minutes!" Victor Snapp announced.

Dad and I headed back to the dugout.

"You learned all of that balloon stuff from one book?" I asked him.

"Some of it," said Dad. "The rest I figured out by looking at it. And the climbing part I learned as a kid. We had a big pine tree out back. And your red binder is in the toolbox."

"I know. Thanks." As soon as we were in the dugout, I took it out. "Which card did Rick tell you to get?" I asked him.

"A fellow named Jim Bunning."

"Right." I spotted the card on the first page.

Bunning wore a Phillies cap and looked like he meant business.

"Did he pitch a perfect game?" I asked Dad.

"Don't ask me," said Dad. "The only Jim Bunning I know was a U.S. senator."

new Varmint pitcher was on the mound. He threw a few warm-up pitches before Tommy Harris came to the plate. Tommy got a base hit, but then Myung Young grounded into a double play. Mike Stammer lined out to third, and the inning was over.

"Finally!" Lance stood up and stretched. "I hope my arm hasn't cooled off too much."

"You'll be fine," said Zeke.

"Hey, Lance! This is for luck." I handed him the Jim Bunning baseball card.

Lance nodded at it. "Perfect!" he said.

He realized what he'd said and grinned. "That's right—I said *perfect*. It's a *perfectly* good word, after all." Lance pocketed the card and headed for the mound. He winked at me, then turned back and shouted to the dugout. "I'm going to finish this *perfect* game," he announced. "Then I'm going to have a *perfect* cup of coffee. Chad, start a new pot now because this won't take long."

I went into the locker room and eyed the coffee machine. Clearly, I had to clean it first. I unscrewed the basket and dumped the damp coffee grounds in the trash.

"Just look at that thing!"

I turned around. My dad was peering into the coffeemaker. He undid the metal rod and held it up to the light. "Young man, get me my tools."

"Dad, you know my name," I reminded him as I handed him the toolbox.

"Maybe so," he said. "Now go to the food stand and find me a big jug of vinegar."

"That sounds like a weird recipe," I said, but off I went.

When I got back, swinging half a gallon of white vinegar, Dad had the bottom of the coffee machine off. He whistled while he worked at something with a screwdriver.

"You can go watch the game," he said. "This will take a while."

I got back out in time to see Lance end the inning with a strikeout. He strode off the mound while the crowd went wild.

"Did you see that, guys?" the pitcher shouted. "I still have a perfect game going!" He came into the dugout. "Eight innings. Zero hits, zero walks, and zero errors."

"Shh!" said Sammy. "Don't jinx it."

"Jinx, schminx," said Lance. "Didn't you ever hear of Jim Bunning?"

"I heard of him," said Sammy. "What about him?"

"He pitched a perfect game once—and he blabbed the entire time," said Lance. "I had forgotten about that until Chad gave me this card. Bunning jinxed his own game and still got through it. Kind of makes me think the whole jinx thing is silly . . . Great choice, Chad! Perfect, even."

"Thanks. It was my uncle Rick's idea."

I hadn't known that about Jim Bunning, but Uncle Rick was like a walking baseball encyclopedia.

"Bunning or not, I don't like it," Sammy muttered.

"Here's to staying perfect," said Tommy,

trading a high five with Lance. "It's already the most perfect game I ever saw."

"Perfect or not," said Teddy, "whatever happens, Lance, you were awesome."

"This is the best thing I've seen since Sammy stole that base," said Wayne.

"Rarest thing I've seen since I turned that unassisted triple play," said Mike. Everybody looked at him. "Well, technically, that's even rarer," he reminded them.

"Enough!" said Grumps. We all turned to look at him. He stood up, and I swear he was the reddest I'd ever seen him. I thought he was about to blow up, but he spoke softly and evenly. "You need three more outs," he reminded Lance. "Until you get them, there's nothing perfect about this game. I've seen 'em get away after eight innings more times than I can count. And I've seen 'em get away after twenty-six outs on three different occasions." He squinted at Lance. "You don't count your outs before the chickens hatch."

"I know, Mr. Humboldt."

"All right, then." Grumps nodded, then turned to the team and shouted, "Is somebody going to go up there and bat, or do I have to do it myself?"

"It's my turn!" said Sammy. I handed him his bat. He went to the plate as fast as he could, which, because it was Sammy, wasn't that fast.

"How's that coffee coming along?" Lance whispered.

"It'll take a while," I told him. "I'm using the vinegar method."

"Never heard of it, but I can't wait to try it," Lance said. "Just so long as I can have a cup when I'm done serving up this perfect game."

• • •

The Porcupines scored a couple more runs, but the crowd was just waiting for the top of the ninth. They started clapping when Lance went out to pitch.

The clapping slowed down when he went into his windup and then let loose when the ball flew out of his hand. The Varmints' first batter swung right away and grounded out, but the second batter took a long time. He took a couple of pitches, then fouled off a bunch. Lance was still cool, zipping pitch after pitch over the plate until he finally got strike three. The crowd cheered.

Everybody stood up for the last batter. The Varmints sent in a pinch hitter, an old-timer who was even older than Wayne Zane. He had a droopy mustache and looked a bit like a hero from a Western movie. His face had no expression. He didn't seem to know, or care, that he was the only one standing between Lance Pantaño and a perfect game.

The batter took one pitch for a strike, and another for a ball. He hit the third pitch so hard that it flew like a missile down the third base line. For about one-tenth of a second it looked like the jinx had finally kicked in . . . but then Tommy Harris stuck out his glove and caught the ball.

The crowd went wild! They stomped and cheered and hooted and waved their hats in the air. The Porcupines crowded around Lance to pat him on the back, and then they carried him off the field. He had to come back nine or ten times and wave his cap at the fans. The last time, he made the entire team go out with him, because it was their perfect game too. It belonged to all the Pines, every one of them.

We could smell coffee brewing when we reached the locker room.

"Just got it started," said Dad. "I used the vinegar to clean the machine, fixed the pump, and tightened a few screws."

The coffee machine was purring.

"Is this thing even on?" Wayne asked. He tapped the side of the machine. It trembled and gasped a little steam.

"The light's on," said Sammy. "Leave it alone."

The coffee was done by the time Lance had showered and dressed.

"I don't know about adding that vinegar," he said. He turned the tap, and coffee gurgled into his cup. He tasted it.

"It's a miracle what you did with this machine," Lance said to my dad. "But the batboy makes better coffee."

Dylan got back from the other locker room, carrying a new balloon porcupine. This one really did look like a porcupine. Its quills angled back the right way instead of sticking out all over.

"Spike made you another one?" I asked.

"Yep," he said. "I think it's the best one yet."

"I didn't even get a balloon animal today," I said.

"I waited in line for it. There were about a hundred kids in front of me. But I had to do *something* while the crowd cheered for ninety minutes straight."

"I'm the bigger Porcupines' fan. Why did

Spike keep giving me monkeys and giraffes and crocodiles instead of the Pines' mascot?"

"Chad," said Dad.

"Yeah?"

"No, not you. Chad the country. All of those animals live in the African savanna, where the nation of Chad is."

"Ah, of course."

Abby was a great mascot, but she was also a good student. She remembered geography class better than I did. We studied many of the countries in Africa, but I forgot them all after we took the test.

"Anyway," said Dylan, "I really wanted a souvenir from today's game. Something to remember it."

"Yep," I said. "Nothing is better than a perfect game."

"Oh, the perfect game was OK," he said.

"But I saw a hot-air balloon crash onto the field during the seventh inning stretch. That's what I was talking about."

"Hmm. Yeah, that was something." I had to remind myself sometimes that Dylan just didn't get baseball.

"Just joshing you, man," Dylan said. "I was talking about the perfect game. That was the coolest thing ever. And you know what's neat? In every single game, the pitcher has a shot at a perfect game. Anything can happen, right? If we keep working for the Pines, we could even see another one!"

"Sure," I said. "That's what's fun about the game. Anything can happen."

"Except one thing," added Dylan. "There's no chance that anyone will ever be eaten by a bear. That's another reason I like baseball."

About the Author

Kurtis Scaletta's previous books include *Mudville*, which *Booklist* called "a gift from the baseball gods" and named one of their 2009 Top 10 Sports Books for Youth. Kurtis lives in Minneapolis with his wife and son and some cats. He roots for the Minnesota Twins and the Saint Paul Saints. Find out more about him at www.kurtisscaletta.com.

About the Artist

Eric Wight was an animator for Disney, Warner Bros., and Cartoon Network before creating the critically acclaimed *Frankie Pickle* graphic novel series. He lives in Doylestown, Pennsylvania, and is a diehard fan of the Philadelphia Phillies and the Lehigh Valley Iron Pigs. You can check out all the fun he is having at www.ericwight.com.

Come on into the **topps**®
Reading
Clubhouse!

Check out these other winning titles in the Topps League Story series featuring Chad, Dylan, Spike, and the Pine City Porcupines.

Can shortstop Mike Stammer

really be *jinxed?*

If DH Sammy Solaris wants to steal,

he'd better run . . . *faster!*

titles from

Who caught Teddy "the Bear" Larrabee's
birthday hit—and will they give it back?